Dedicated to our
granddaughter

December's child with slate blue eyes; her smile lights up our home
Playful as a puppy, curious as a kitten…as she toddles from room to room
Sandy brown hair, with cheeks so fair that really suit her face
Likes exploring every nook and cranny, as if she owns the place
Happy to see you but just for a while; an inquisitive mind hungering to know
All the things she wants to see, feel and touch; no matter where she goes
A child who smiles, then waves to you, after your gaze has turned away
She babbles in words yet unspoken, urging you to come follow and play

- D.C. Donahue

Keira in the Mirror

Requests for permission to make copies of any part of the work should be submitted online
at info@mascotbooks.com or mailed to Mascot Books, 560 Herndon Parkway #120,
Herndon, VA 20170.

PRT1214A

Printed in the United States
Library of Congress Control Number: 2014919279
ISBN-13: 978-1-62086-902-4

www.mascotbooks.com

Keira
in
the
Mirror

D.C. Donahue

Illustrated by Cindy Strosser

Who's that little girl, with the sandy brown hair, staring back at me?

Laughing as she claps her hands while Mommy sings, "So Big"!

She looks so oddly familiar; I know I've seen her here before.

Hmm…was it in the hallway mirror or perhaps the one hanging on my door?

I catch her looking back at me;
almost everywhere I go.

I see her face in things I pass
wearing familiar clothes.

I've seen her in the bathroom mirror, watching Daddy as he shaves.

Then again in Mommy's room as she combs her hair each day.

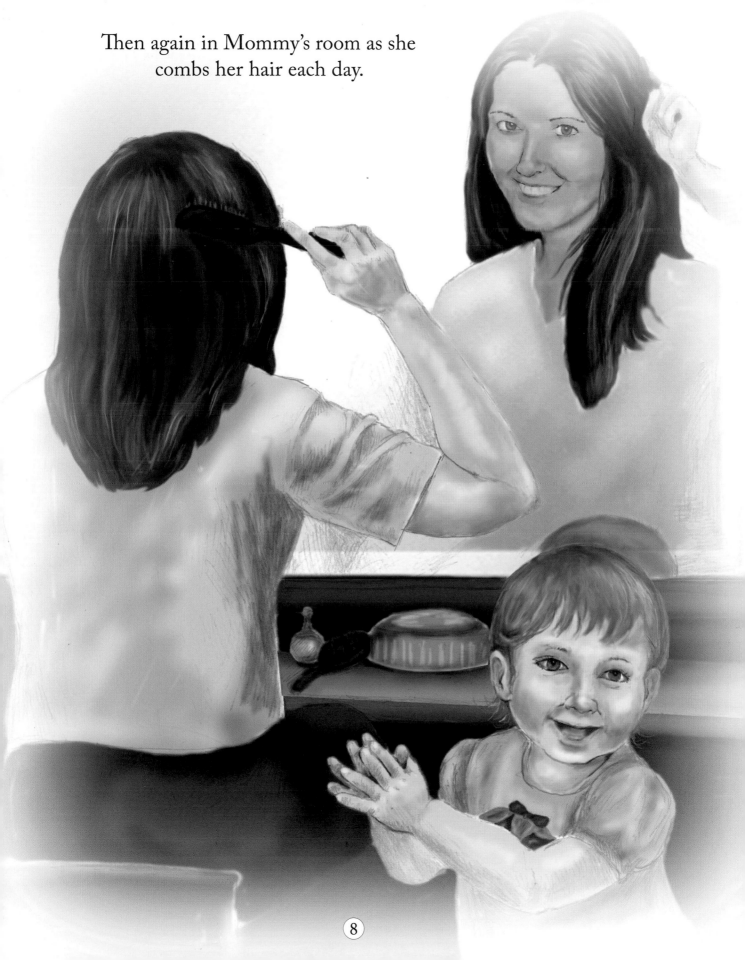

I spot her looking up at me in
Mimi's pots and pans

Which I pulled from her old cupboard to
lend a helping hand.

As Pop-Pop swings me round and round,
we dance about his home.

Hmm… The only time I don't see her is
when I am in my crib alone.

I see her in the silliest places, foil
birthday balloons and the like.

I even caught her face in the little mirror
while on the back of Daddy's bike.

I try to catch her looking up and down
or to the left and right of me.

But she's as fast as two squirrels running
round and round a tree.

Poof! I look into the grandfather clock
and magically see her face.

Then she's staring back at me in the glass
of the fireplace.

Just as quick, with a funny smile I dart
away towards the stairs.

I look back to see if she is following,
but she has disappeared.

I see her in the mirror in the den as I bang the keys on the piano.

She covers her eyes playing peek-a-boo, just like someone else I know.

Oh! I know now who this girl is,
though she never spoke a word to hear.

With the same eyes, nose, and sandy
hair, it's me, Keira in the mirror!

We hope you enjoyed reading this book to your loved ones. We'd also like to recommend a heartwarming, family, children's Christmas story written by the author and available at most online bookstores:

A Glimpse from Christmas Past
ISBN: 9781481740289

⌇

Please be sure to visit the author's website to find kid's games or post comments and reviews. We would love to hear from you at:
www.dcdonahue.com

⌇

Also coming soon, look for *Where's John Liam? Now I See Him!* a follow up in the series to *Keira in the Mirror.*

Thank you!

-The Donahues

Have a book idea?

Contact us at:

Mascot Books
560 Herndon Parkway
Suite 120
Herndon, VA 20170

info@mascotbooks.com | www.mascotbooks.com

About the Author

The author lived most of his childhood in Southwest Philadelphia during the wonder years. His family moved to its western suburbs where he met and married his wife, Nancy. They've been happily married for many years and still reside in the same community. It is also where they raised their four children, Marie, Danny, Kate, and Michael. They now have grandchildren who they enjoy very much and are the author's inspiration.